Contents

Chapter One

Elegance Of The Falls

Celestal's flowing, purple mane glowed in the eerie sunlight, shades of light green dappling across the Jade fields.

"Another beautiful morning on Unicorn Island " she murmured to herself.

The elegant, golden sun shone on Celestal's face, beating across the deep, shady trees. Unicorn Island was a mystical place where unicorns, Pegasi, Alicorns, and ponies were all living.

"*I should go back to my cottage to get some bread for the*

Unicorn Magic

Celestal's Midsummer Rose

Mia Kenyon

Coming Soon:

Unicorn Magic:
Snowflake's Midwinter Magic

Unicorn Magic:
Eliza's Crystal Star

ducks," Celestal said to herself. "*They're surely hot and hungry.*" Trotting back, she saw the sights of Midsummer just on Unicorn Island.

She darted across the plains, the wind blowing in her elegant, beautiful face.

Her mane swiftly swayed behind her, galloping across the thin layers of thick strands of grass.

Her village, Bridle Falls, was a peaceful living place near Rainbow Falls, a giant waterfall that dropped three miles down.

When she got to the outskirts, Celestal halted to a stop. Her cottage was nearby, but she was so out of breath from all the galloping, Celestal decided it was a good idea to trot from now on.

She started a peaceful, slow trot around the village, taking in the sights and sounds. Soon enough, she had successfully arrived at her cottage door.

Trotting in, she opened her creaky cupboard door. She grabbed the seed loaf, took two slices and ripped them into small pieces before placing them all in a plastic zipper bag to keep the bits of bread fresh.

She zoomed across the plains, making the most of the wonderful experience. Halfway there, something big and colourful swooped above her.

It was Adrenaline, the sports Pegasus! She was known for her amazing sports routines and for her famous flying conducting skills.

"*Hello, Adrenaline. Are you out doing some flying exercises for the morning?*" Celestal asked curiously. "*Well, I'm only giving my wings a stretch before lunch*," Adrenaline replied.

Then Celestal thought. *I have to feed the ducks!* she reminded herself remarkably in her head.

"*Adrenaline, it was nice to chat, but I need to go somewhere important*" Celestal quickly replied before the conversation could go any further. "*Okay, byeeeee!*" Adrenaline speed-talked. Then off she darted.

Celestal knew she needed to carry on, or it would be no lunch at midday! Quickly, she tried to sprint to the lake, as there was a huge hill and this was a tough circuit.

But she **had** to do it. Even if she was completely worn out by the time she was there, those ducks had to be fed and she needed to return home in time for her lunch.

So off she galloped, bounding through the trees and weaving in and out of branches. Halfway up the hill, her hooves were shrouded in sweat.

At one point, her hooves were so slippy, she nearly rolled backwards down the hill! After that frightening incident, Celestal ran instead of sprinting.

The wind blew on her pearl pink nuzzle, freshness entering her body.
The puffy, pale lavender clouds floated gently through the open skies. “Beautiful!” she exclaimed.

Racing up the hill, she soon realized she was at the lake. Ducks called harminious tunes, knowing Celestal was going to feed them. She made her way over, ducks following her one by one.

“*Wow*!” cried Celestal, ducks flapping their wings around her. It was such a glorious sight!

Then, all of a sudden, a young, fluffy, yellow duckling set off downstream! Luckily, Celestal spotted him. “*No! Not a duckling*!” she cried.

Even though she was scared, that young bird’s life

depended on her.
So with that thought over, she plunged in. Floating downstream, she looked down. They were about to go over Rainbow Falls!

Celestal closed her eyes with fear. They were about to plummet down the 3 mile drop! Her life flashed in front of her eyes.

All of a sudden, crowds of ponies from the village gathered around the huge, colossal waterfall. Her mother and father were there too! With one gulp of fright, Celestal and the Duckling fell!

They screamed, dropping down from the three mile height. Swiftly and softly, they landed in the pool of water below. They were soaked to the bone, hearts beating fast but unharmed!

Climbing out, Celestal shook her mane and her rescued duckling waddled off shaking his tail feathers.

The villagers were relieved to know that they were safe. After all the excitement, they had a drink from the pool.

Suddenly their eyes changed into an Emerald glow of green. Celestal was suspicious of this strange phenomenon. What was going on, she thought?

Chapter Two

A Message To The Queen

On the way back home, Celestal heard her parents arguing over something. She tried to listen in to find out. But of course, it was no use. They just pushed her out of the way.

This is not like my parents, Celestal thought. *They would never argue without telling me what's up.*

Celestal thought long and hard about it. *These constant arguments and the green glowing eyes seem serious. I'd better tell the Queen.*

Whilst her parents weren't looking, Celestal rushed back to her cottage. Once she was safely inside, she started scanning through the bookshelves for a special spellbook she needed.

"*A-ha!*" Celestal exclaimed, picking up a spellbook called 'Firework Signals'. Suddenly, she saw her parents approaching the cottage.

Celestal had to escape. She didn't want to be involved in the scuffle her parents were in. Scanning the room, she spotted an open window.

Quickly, she climbed onto a chest drawer, squeezed out of the top, and ran off. She was glad she had escaped.

Her heart pounding, Celestal raced up the huge hill and made it to the very top. Turning in the opposite direction of the pond she opened the book.

Flipping through the blotchy, inky pages, she stopped abruptly at the spell that said 'Firework message'. "*Perfect*," said Celestal, grinning to herself.

Then she read the page. It was very simple for Celestal to understand, as she was a very talented unicorn in advanced magic class.

Knowing what to do, she got her magic up and running. A golden, eerie glow surrounded her horn as she carefully wrote out the message in rose gold fiery sparks.

It said: *Queen Titana, Please help me, love from Celestal.*

The magic made stars shoot out of her horn making the message visible to Queen Titana. Once the spell was complete, Celestal lowered her horn. The glow disappeared and her horn was back to normal.

In the distance, Queen Titana spotted the glow from the firework letters reflecting on her glass window. Stepping out, she spotted Celestal's signal.

"*Oh my,*" the Queen muttered to herself. "*Celestal really does need my help if she sent a firework signal message.*"

Meanwhile, Celestal was resting from the spell she had cast a while ago. Feeling a bit dazed, she stood up. "*Maybe I'll read the rest of that magic book for emergencies*" said Celestal responsibly.

And so Celestal did. Instead of flipping through all the pages, she read carefully. One was a sparkle spell that exploded once touched.

“That’s useful if I need to attack an evil being” Celestal said thoughtfully to herself.

Meanwhile, Queen Titana was thinking out loud. “*Maybe I need to transport Celestal here to have a talk in closer detail*” she said. “*Good idea, ma’m*” said one of the royal pony guards.

“*You're right there*,” replied Queen Titana. “*So I should.*”

So that’s what she did. Casting a spell with her horn, soon, Celestal felt quite tingly. “*What’s happening*?” she cried.

Soon, the talented Unicorn was shrouded in a blue coloured mist, feeling rather tingly, much more than she had done before.

Soon, the mist had faded and she was somewhere completely different than the hillside. She was in Queen Titana’s Cloud Castle!

Celestal couldn’t believe it. Why was she here? Who sent her? Celestal realised her signal must have been seen. Then, she turned around. Behind her was Queen Titana!

"*Well hello, Celestal. Nice to see you. Why did you send that signal*?" The Queen asked politely. "*Well, something doesn't seem right in my village*," Celestal replied.

"*Everyone except me has green glowing eyes and they keep arguing and scuffling with one another. It's very unusual.*"

"*This does sound rather serious," Queen Titania remarked. "I'm sure I definitely know what's wrong here Celestal. Follow me.*"

Queen Titana took Celestal down a long, lilac, spiral staircase. It finished in the old library.

Celestal sat down on a purple velvet stool, whilst Queen Titana took a thick dusty book down from one of the shelves and placed it on an oak table infront of where Celestal was sitting.

"*Celestal, listen. Here's the story of Midsummer's night*" Queen Titana explained.

Opening the book the Queen began to read the legend of the curse out loud to Celestal and she sat and listened.

Chapter Three

The Midsummer's Curse

"Many years ago, the water from the Rainbow Falls pool was poisoned by sunlight. The beings were made so thirsty that they drank from the pool. Within moments of their lips touching the water their eyes started to glow a bright Emerald green." began Queen Titana.

"*That's exactly what happened when the ponies drank it before*" Celestal said. "*That's right,*" said The Queen. "*Let me continue with the story.*"

"*Whilst this was happening one pony splashed down into the cool blue water and became immune from the curse of the green eyes. Once their eyes changed colour all the other ponies and beings started to argue.*"

"*That's right, it's what's happening now*" said Celestal.
"*Okay,*" said Queen Titana. "*The story has it that the immune pony saved the ponies by picking a sparkle rose at midnight and everyone was free from the curse.*"

"*So is that the story?*" questioned Celestal. "*So it is,*" said Queen Titana. "*But that's not all. Legend has it that if the rose isn't picked, Unicorn Island will split in half and a feud will begin.*"

"*But Queen Titana, I need to pick the rose because I splashed down from the waterfall before I messaged you.*" said Celestal.

"*You're right there Celestal,*" replied Queen Titana. "*You must. Otherwise Unicorn Island will be a place of war and not hope.*"

"*Well, I certainly don't want to be living in the middle of a war,*" Celestal said. "*I will do it, Queen Titana, for the sake of Unicorn Island!*"

"*The quest is yours, Celestal, be brave and keep that positive attitude,*" replied Queen Titanta. "*We have no time to lose, we must get you prepared straight away.*"

"*First, your Majesty, I need some lunch*," said Celestal. "*I've not eaten yet*." "*Well, you can have some with me*," Queen Titana kindly said. "*Thank you*," replied Celestal.

So off the pair went to the Royal Buffet Room. But when they got there, all the Guards had green eyes and were in a huge scuffle.

"*Oh my*!" cried Queen Titana. "*This is not like them*." "*Maybe it's the Midsummer's Curse*!" exclaimed Celestal. "*What type of water do you drink*?" "*Rainbow Falls spring water*," Queen Titana worriedly replied.

"*But it's poisoned*!" cried Celestal, anxiously. "*They have the curse*!" "*I need to warn the rest of the island with a firework signal, or it'll spread*!" replied Queen Titana.

Queen Titana came to all the windows and did a firework signal out of all of them. It said:

'Beware of The Rainbow Falls pool! Do not drink from it! Yours, Queen Titana.'

After Queen Titana had finished and lowered her horn, Celestal asked a question. "*Queen Titana, how are we going to get lunch at this rate*?" she asked.
"*Maybe we could go to the kitchen*," suggested Queen Titana hopefully. "*Good idea*," said Celestal happily. "*Let's go*!" And so they did.

After their meal, Celestal said: "*Queen Titana, while we're in here, shall we make some food for my journey*?" "*Of Course, Celestal*," replied Queen Titana. "*I don't want you to be hungry*."

They made some honey drizzle salad with some tomatoes, lettuce, cucumber, rocket, cream, and of course, glitter bee honey.

They put it into a tupperware tub and sealed it. After that, Queen Titana magicked up a chocolate crunch bar for her and explained why: "*The guards are scuffling over the last one in the pantry, so I've magicked you one instead. Okay?*" "*I'm fine with that, thank you,*" replied Celestal.

The pair put the food in Celestal's saddlebag, placing it next to the spellbook she had brought with her. Queen Titana noticed the book and asked, "*Is that how you sent me that signal,*"? "*Yes that's how I messaged you,*" replied Celestal, glancing down at the leather cover. "*You must be a talented young unicorn with incredible power, Celestal*" said The Queen.

"*Well, I must have incredible powers,*" admitted Celestal. "*I'm the top student in my Advanced Magic Class.*"

"*Celestal, you must get going now, time is running out!*"

exclaimed Queen Titana. "*Unicorn Island needs you Celestal. Go*!"

Celestal was given a map so she knew the way. After saying goodbye to Queen Titana, she opened the castle drawbridge and stepped out.

Her adventure for Unicorn Island had begun!

Chapter Four

Journey through Neverfree

After Celestal stepped down from the wooden drawbridge, she glanced down at her map. "*So, the Sparkle Rose is on Mount Red Vine, is it*?" firmly confirmed Celestal.

But then, looking closely, she realised the line went through Neverfree - a bitter, horrible, tangly forest that sat around Mount Red Vine.

Celestal gulped with fright. There were all sorts in there! But Celestal had made a promise to Queen Titana that she would pick that Sparkle Rose at Midnight and save Unicorn Island!

Celestal saw that she had to go over a small bridge by Rainbow River, and that would lead her straight into Neverfree.

"*Perfect*!" exclaimed Celestal excitedly. "*I can get there nice and quickly*." She galloped over the mounds of grass, the texture embroidering her hooves.

As she reached the small, rough bridge, the sound of water rushing came into her small, delicate ears. The shades of blue in the fresh, clean water eclipsed against each other.

Celestal crossed over, the tweets and birdsong of Sparrows freshening the air. After Celestal stepped off, in front of her was Neverfree!

Thick, tangling vines wrapped around the tall, colossal trees. The dark green shadows shone over the brownish-red grass, dampening the soft feel.

Celestal entered the dull, dingy forest, her nuzzle screwing up in disgust. But she had to at least make it. Celestal took her watch out of her saddlebag. It read 2:45.

She was doing good with time. She had more than eight hours to find Mount Red Vine and to pick the rose at Midnight.

She trotted on, the blue skies left behind her mane, the forest green atmosphere entering her eyes. Shades of green, turquoise, and aqua were everywhere around her.

Celestal went on, looking at all the messy, thorny wildlife around her. She thought all the plants were beautiful and exotic in Neverfree.

Celestal knew that she had to tread carefully, or she could step on something she wasn't meant to step on.

Just then, something coiled around her back right hoof. It was Strangleweed! Then it went and coiled around her back left hoof.

Celestal felt she couldn't move. Realizing something must be gripping onto her, she turned around. The Strangleweed was gripping onto her back hooves!

Then a new piece wrapped around both of her front hooves. It looked like she was completely and utterly trapped!

Then a thoughtful idea popped into Celestal's head. The spellbook! With her teeth, she opened her leather saddlebag. Then, she grabbed the book.

She controlled the book and pages with her horn. She flipped through it all until she managed to find the exploding sparkle spell. She had a quick look at it before placing the spell book back in her saddlebag.

Then she got her magic up and running once again. This time, her eerie, golden glow turned into pale orange sparkles that floated down onto the pieces of Strangleweed.

Then, the verocious vines snapped in half. Celestal was finally free! She hoped there were definitely going to be no more incidents like that.

Celestal knew that now she was free, she needed to successfully continue her journey to Mount Red Vine with no more clumsy incidents.

After, she started her hooves up again and began to trot forwards once more. She went past wild, growing bushes and beautiful, exotic flowers.

Her mane sparkled with the spell she had just cast. It looked beautiful and seemed to brighten her path up. It was very useful for going through dark places.

Suddenly, Celestal heard a bird's call. Then, something rock-like swooped in and one by one, more came in, landing in front of the unicorn.

The creatures were Gargoyle Falcons.

Chapter Five

The Gargoyle Falcons

"*Well, well, well, what do we have here*?" the first one piped up, looking at the frightened Unicorn. "*Is it food*?" asked another, looking hungry. "*No, you silly fool, it's not food*!" said the third one.

Then Celestal said: "*Hello. Who are you three*?" "*Oh, we're the Falcon Brothers, us three*," said the first. "*We're the finest hunters in the forest*," said the second.

"*Stop bragging*!" said the third. "*Well, it's nice to know you three, but I need to be off*" said Celestal. "*Not yet, you don't*," said the first Gargoyle Falcon.

"*Why*?" asked Celestal suspiciously. "*Because* **we** *want some food first*" said the second. "*Why are you always so hungry*?" asked the third.

"*Be quiet*!" instructed the second. "*Our master wants to speak*." "*So will you help us*?" asked the first to Celestal. "*Of course*!" she said. "*I'd always help any animal in need*."

"*Good then*," said the second. "*I'm starving*." "*Do you have to say that*," said the third.

"*Let's head forwards,*" suggested the first. "*There's always lots of food in the heart of the forest.*" "*Good idea,*" said the third.

"*I'm hungry,*" moaned the second, clutching his tummy. "*We know*!" chimed the first and third.

"*Well, you unicorn, what are we waiting for, let's go*!" announced the first, also the leader.

So Celestal followed the three deeper and deeper in, until they were in the heart of Neverfree, full of exciting beings. "*Wow,*" examined Celestal. "*This is so elegant*!"

Birds of all kinds swooped in and out of beds of pretty

bluebells. Shades of turquoise dappled over the murky, green river. The Gargoyle Falcons also seemed to like it too.
The second falcon started chewing on leaves he was so starving! "*Get off those*!" stubbornly shouted the third. "*They're not edible*!"

"*Ooops*," replied the second, swallowing his first mouthful. "*Eww, that's gross*!" said the first. "*Stop it you two*!" grudged the third.

"*You three don't seem to get along so well*," said Celestal. "*It's time for you guys to learn how to at least get along with each other*."

The three falcons stopped bickering at once. "*What do you mean by 'get along*?" asked the first. "*He means be nice to each other, you silly gargoyle*," said the third. "*How can we do that*?" muffled the second, swallowing a mouthful of purple berries.

"*Don't chew with your mouth open, it's rude*!" pointed out the third. "*See, you two just bickered there*!" said Celestal sternly. "*Enough is enough for you three! Stop it now*!"

They were speechless. All of a sudden, the first Gargoyle Falcon set its eyes on Celestal. She realized the Gargoyle was doing the stare!

Celestal fixed her eyes on the Gargoyle Falcon. She knew she couldn't blink, or she would be solid stone. Celestal looked into the bird's glowing, red eyes. She didn't blink once for more than five minutes. Then, the falcon suddenly blinked.

"*Hey*!" he shouted at Celestal angrily. "*You ruined my stare*!" "*Well you were the one who blinked, honest*" Celestal said truthfully.

Then the second Gargoyle Falcon stopped chewing and said: "*She's right, that unicorn. You did blink, after all.*"

Celestal couldn't believe it. She'd made one of the Gargoyle Falcons stop bickering. Excitement and pleasure filled her heart with glory.
Then, the other one stopped bickering too, and was also honest. Celestal gave them some purple berries and sparkle honey for dessert, as they were so good.

"*You two, will you show me where the foot of Mount Red Vine is, please*? " asked Celestal. "*Of course, unicorn. We will*" said the two falcons.

So they walked through to the edge of Neverfree, taking in the lovely sounds. Soon, they had reached the foot of the mountain. She said thank you to them both. As soon as they were gone, she took a deep breath.

She was ready to tackle Mount Red Vine!

Chapter Six

Climbing Mount Red Vine

Celestal let out her breath and put one hoof onto the steep, slippery surface of the Mountain. It felt cold, wet, and drippy. Before she went any further, she checked her watch. It said 7:30.

Celestal realized she didn't have long. She only had four and a half hours to climb up the mountain and to pick the rose.

She would have to skip dinner and supper for the sake of her homeland. But she didn't mind. She could eat an early breakfast instead. Much better.

The brave unicorn gripped onto a rock with her front right hoof and then the left. And then she started the exact same process with her back hooves as well.

The moss felt cold, wet and squelchy, but her hooves were already used to it because she had been walking through Neverfree. The rock and charcoal was sharp underneath her delicate, sparkly, glittery hooves. She knew they were definitely going to be sore by the time she was there.

All of a sudden, she saw something infront of her. It was a vision of Queen Titana!

"*Hello Celestal. I see you're on Mount Red Vine. Be careful, there are some harmful beings up there. See you soon Celestal. Bye*" said the vision.

Celestal had really been warned. Now, she would have to really watch her step whilst she was climbing. Quickly, Celestal turned her head to the right. Since one mound had ended there was a small porch carved out the Mountainside to cross over.

She climbed down, and once she was down enough, she managed to spot that the bridge was hanging down!

Celestal knew there was another way across the gap.

She finished climbing down and stepped onto the porch. Then, she noticed some red vines just by the side of her. And just like that, an idea popped into Celestal's head.

She grabbed the thorny, sharp plant and swung across the gap. It felt like gliding!

The wind blew aside her purple mane. After that special few moments she successfully and safely landed on the other porch. Then, she continued to climb upwards.

The freshness entered her body, breathing in through her

soft, gentle nuzzle. Suddenly wind gales started to pick up. Celestal felt that she needed a rest, so she climbed up to the top of the mound. On the top of it were some unprotected chicks!

Celestal climbed to the top to protect them. Like Queen Titana had said, there were many predators on Mount Red Vine.

Soon, Celestal spotted a huge silhouette of a bird. Their mother had come home! She hoped that this bird was friendly. Celestal didn't want to be kicked off the mound!

Once their mother had landed, the huge bird had a smile on her beak. "*Hello*," the friendly being said. "*Thank you for looking after my chicks*." "*Oh, you're welcome*," Celestal blushed unexpectedly. "*Anyway, what type of bird are you*?"

"*I'm a Roc, but a very friendly one*," replied the Roc. "*So are these your chicks*?" asked Celestal. "*Of course they are*," replied Roc.

"*Can I have a ride please*?" asked Celestal. "*Of course you can*," replied Roc. "*Climb on my back and I'll take you over to that bridge over and up there*."

"*Thank you*," said Celestal. "*If you need help, I'll be able to sense it*," replied Roc. So with that, Celestal climbed onto the Roc's huge, bumpy back. As soon as the chicks had hopped on, the Roc took off. Her big, rocky wings brushed against Celestal's face.

She really was flying! Celestal had never flown on a huge, friendly bird's back before. She loved it! In a couple of minutes, they had landed near the bridge.

As soon as Celestal had hopped off, the Roc took off once again. "*Thank you*!" called Celestal. But in the blink of an eye, the female bird had gone.

Then, Celestal began to cross the bridge. It was made of rickety, redwood.

There were no ropes along the side, so she would have

to keep her balance. All of a sudden, three familiar birds circled her. It was the Gargoyle Falcons!

"*I don't get it*!" exclaimed Celestal. "*I thought I reformed you*!" "*It was my stare that controlled those two*," said the first. "*Yes, he so did*," said the second and third.

"*You are not picking that rose*," said the first. "*We saw that vision of Titana's she sent you*" *I need to get away*, thought Celestal. But she couldn't. Celestal was trapped.

What was she going to do?

Chapter Seven

Roc To The Rescue

The Gargoyle Falcons circled Celestal, the unicorn moving in each time they got closer. She was trapped! It was probably 10:00 by now. It wasn't long until Midnight! Then, a silhouette soared above Celestal's head. As it soared down towards her, she thought it was another Gargoyle Falcon. But it wasn't. It was the Roc being!

Celestal sighed with relief. If it had been another Gargoyle Falcon it would be game over for her! Celestal waved her hooves wildly so the bird could notice.

But the Gargoyle Falcons screeched with fear. "*Eek*!" cried the first. "*It's a rocwurzel*!" shouted the third. "*Fly for your lives*!" cried the second.

"*Wait, you two silly gargoyles*!" bossed the first. "*We don't know what it is yet.*" "*Fine*," said the third.

"*Celestal*!" called the Roc excitedly. "*It's so good to see you*!" "*I know*," said Celestal with a warm smile and a glow in her eyes.

"*We need to escape from these three, before they do their stoney stare*," replied the Roc knowingly.

"*But how?*" questioned Celestal.

"*With a little Roc knowledge*," said the warm- hearted bird. "*You'll see*." So Celestal followed her instructions carefully.

"*First, you need to start your stare at them*," said the Roc. "*Then, make the Falcons stare back. And Finally, make them blink*." Celestal did just that. She started off a strong stare for the falcons to look at.

The three were intrigued. "*What is that unicorn doing*," asked the first. "*The stare, of course*," said the second. "*Let's join in*," said the third.

So they did. Next, Celestal thought up a way for them to blink. "*Roc, will you let me pick a feather off your wing*," whispered Celestal, winking. "*Yup*," said the Roc. "*Of course*." So that's what Celestal did.

Whilst the Falcons were busy staring, she carefully picked a delicate feather from the Roc's right wing. Then, Celestal tickled their beaks.

"*Hee hee hee hee*," laughed the first. "*Achoo*!" went the second. "*Stop it*!" said the third. "*I'm going to turn you to stone*." Then, with that, the three blinked. "*Noooo*!" they shouted and then immediately froze.

Solid stone and rock covered their bodies, wings and beaks. The last word they said was: "*Hel. . .!*" before their beaks turned to stone.

"*Yes*!" Celestal exclaimed with delight. "*We did it*!" shouted the Roc. Then they high fived each other in celebration.

Celestal took her watch from her saddlebag. It read 11:30! "*Oh no*!" said Celestal anxiously. "*Sorry, Roc, but I really need to continue on my quest and make up for the lost time*"

"*That's okay, Celestal,*" said the Roc. "*You can have another ride on my back if you like.*" "*Oh, yes please!*"

Celestal said delightfully.

"*Come on then, on you get*," said the Roc, helping Celestal up. Once she was firmly on, the pair wooshed into the night sky. Celestal was in the air once again!

"*Whee*!" cried Celestal, the night air blustering in her face. "*This is so refreshing*!" They went around corners and swerved in and out of branches.

The Roc knew Celestal liked the ride very much and knew magic was not her only passion, flying was one too!

Soon, the Roc came to a stop.

"*Sorry, Celestal, but I can't go above cloud level, so you must make the rest of the expedition on foot,*" explained the Roc. "*That's okay," said Celestal softly. "I know now.*"

After Celestal had said thank you, the Roc beat her huge, feathery wings and zoomed off into the starry night sky.

So Celestal climbed past the misty, blue clouds and up the steep, rock slopes. This was worse than the huge hill back at home!

Soon enough, and with lots of perseverance and patience, she finally reached the top of the rough, hard mountain. Magnificently, Celestal had made it up Mount Red Vine!

It was a big achievement for one small pony. At the top, Celestal noticed a glimmering, shimmering, rainbow-coloured flower.

It was the sparkle rose!

Chapter Eight

Midnight Strike

Celestal checked her watch for the time. 11:58! It was only two minutes until it was midnight! Celestal realised she would have to pick that rose fast!

She stepped up to the magical plant, her hooves tingled as she got nearer. Celestal didn't know if she was able to pick the rose in time to save Unicorn Island.

But then, the unicorn remembered who she'd met and how they had helped her on the treacherous journey she had survived.

How Queen Titana helped her get prepared, how the

Gargoyle Falcons helped her find the heart of Neverfree forest, and how the Roc had helped her escape the stoney eyed Gargoyles and to reach the higher parts of the Mountain.

Celestal couldn't give up now. Those positive thoughts circling her head, she was ready to uproot the rose. Even though it was delicate and precious, she had to do it.

She trotted over to the rose, and when she reached it, she knelt down.

She really wished she had brought some safety gloves with her once she saw how sharp the thorns were.

She took one deep breath, and gripped onto the green, thorny stem. Then, she began to slightly pull. She realised it was not going to be dragged from the ground easily.

This time, she tried tugging a little harder. But of course, it didn't come free. *This rose must be stubborn,* thought Celestal.

And for her final try at freeing it from the earth, Celestal pulled it with all her might. Her muscles strained as it finally became free with one more almighty heave!
She glanced down at her watch. It was 12:00 Midnight!
But she then noticed nothing had happened.

But then, an eerie glow filled the rose and the night sky. Something was happening after all! Over Unicorn Island, the arguing was dying down. Green irises in the pupils of beings were fading as well.

Celestal even sent another firework signal to Queen Titana to show it was working! This time it said: *Queen Titana, I did it! I saved Unicorn Island!*

Back at the cloud castle, one of the guards spotted it and woke Queen Titana at once. "*Ma'am*!" he shouted. "*There is a message the unicorn has sent you*!" Queen

Titana woke at once with this news. "*Celestal's done it*!" she exclaimed. "*She's saved Unicorn Island*!"

Meanwhile, back on the bridge, the Gargoyle Falcons unfroze and gave each other compliments. At the Cloud Castle, the guards went on their night shift instead of arguing over sweets.

Everything and everyone on Unicorn Island was finally back to normal!

Celestal's parents were relieved and yet at the same time they were worn out after their argument. They went to sleep straight away, as they needed rest.

Back on Mount Red Vine, Celestal was enjoying the feeling of just being proud. She had never done anything this big and amazing before.

She just sat down and watched the fireworks everyone was setting off. *They must be for pleasure,* thought Celestal. She felt she was being praised by all the kind ponies out there.

A deep thought about the day surrounded her. *Maybe I'm a special and talented unicorn. It's my job to embrace magic.*

Back at the Cloud Castle, Queen Titana was deep in thought. "*Maybe it's time to give Celestal a gift*," she said. "*Like what*?" asked a curious guard.

"*Not like one you give, but one that will stay on her back*," said Queen Titana. "*Oh, that gift given to you*," said the same guard. "*Yes, like that*," replied Queen Titana. "*I think it's time for her, ma'am*," said another guard, seriously looking at her. "*Me too*," said Queen Titana with a smile on her face.

So after the conversation, she got her magic going. It was purple, and very strong. She could feel it was the time for Celestal.

Meanwhile, Celestal was thinking of ways to get down. She was very scared, in case one of them didn't work.

Just when she thought of a good one, a magical energy surrounded her. It was a pastel rainbow mist. All of a sudden, she was transported to somewhere very quiet. Infront of her was Queen Titana. This was strange.

What was happening to her?

Chapter Nine

A Winged Wonder

"*Celestal, it's time*," said Queen Titana softly. "*Time for what*?" asked Celestal. "*A Miracle to change your life forever*," answered Queen Titana hopefully.

"*Am I special, then*?" asked Celestal. "*Very special and unique indeed*," replied Queen Titana. "*And that miracle is about to happen*."

Queen Titana's purple, eerie magical glow surrounded her horn silently and slowly. The magic transported Celestal to a place with visions of her entire life.

Celestal looked back at her humongous journey. From being born and passing her first exam at magic school, to the journey up Mount Red Vine she had just done.

There was certainly a lot to view. She thought about her kind actions and words she had said to everypony.

Once she had a look, something well and truly amazing happened to her. A rainbow glow surrounded her, and was swept up by music notes and sparkle roses.

Then, a voice said to her: "*Celestal now is your time. You are ready for a miracle to happen.*" And with that, she was shadowed by the mist.

Once it faded, she was back in the Cloud Castle, with Queen Titana by her side. "*Celestal, have a look at yourself in that mirror over there. the miracle gift will be obvious,*"

said Queen Titana. So Celestal looked in the mirror and saw she had a beautiful, shiny pair of gossamer wings on her back.

"*Wow!*" exclaimed Celestal. "*My miracle really is on my back.*" "*I know,*" said Queen Titana. "*I've got some on my back, too.*"

"*So am I a princess if I have wings and a horn*?" asked Celestal curiously. "*Of course you are, Celestal,*" said Queen Titana.

"*Wow, that really is special,*" said Celestal with delight, "*I cannot wait until I begin to learn how to use my wings to fly*". "*So it is,*" replied Queen Titana. The pair smiled.

"*You've got a coronation tomorrow, to show that you are a princess*" said Queen Titana. "*Do I really*?" asked Celestal, intrigued.

"*Of course you do,*" said Queen Titana. "*I've had one too. All princesses have one.*" "*I need to get home quickly,*" said Celestal. "*I need a good sleep ready for tomorrow.*" "*And so you do,*" said Queen Titana. "*Do you want me to magic you back?*" "*No thank you,*" said Celestal. "*I'm okay, but thanks for asking*".

"*Well, thank you for saving the island,*" said Queen Titana. "*Otherwise, Unicorn Island would be at war right now.*"

After saying goodbye to Queen Titana, she opened the drawbridge and set off to Bridle Falls, where she was meant to be.

She trotted over the plains, her hooves hurting with exhaustment and her new wings tucked behind her fluttering in the breeze. Celestal was very tired from her

journey, and was starting to become very sleepy. Just then, something called: "*Celestal*! *You're here*!" It was her parents!

"*Why are you out so late*? *Oh my goodness you have wings*?" exclaimed her mother. "*It's a long story, but I'm just glad you're here*!" said Celestal. "*You must be tired*," said her father.

"*Let's get you to bed*," said her mother, giving Celestal a hug. So Celestal and her parents made it back to their cottage in Bridle Falls, each of them tired out from the events of the day.

Celestal's parents helped the tired unicorn into her bed, and made sure her eyes were closed and Celestal was starting to drift into a deep dreamy sleep.

After that, both parents went to bed themselves, smiling at each other about the silly argument they had earlier which they could not remember what they were arguing about.

The next morning was a wonderful bright fresh morning with a golden red and purple sunrise, and Celestal was awakened by beams of sunlight peeking over the distant hills and streaming into her bedroom window. She fluttered out of her bed, stretching her hooves and new wings after a good night's sleep.

The day was turning into a nice, warm, sunny day, perfect for her coronation. She rushed over to her parents' bedroom, waiting to tell them the news that Queen Titana was going to crown her a princess.

Celestal entered her parents bedroom and lightly trotted over to their bed and gently prodded them. "*What is it Celestal*?" asked her mother.

"*It's my coronation day today*!" piped up Celestal, her mother noticing the gossamer wings on her daughter's back.

"*Am I dreaming*?" asked her dad, noticing the same thing.

"*No, you aren't*," said Celestal, winking. "*I really am a princess, don't you remember my wings from yesterday*?"

Chapter Ten

Coronation Day

"*Ah yes the wings now I remember and how on unicorn earth did you get them and change into a princess?*" asked her Mother. "*By being rewarded a gift from Queen Titana for saving Unicorn Island from a terrible curse*," replied Celestal. Her parents glanced at each other thinking, *what an incredible daughter we have*!

"*Let's get you some breakfast, beautiful princess girl*," said her mother. "*its ok I can do it*" said Celestal as she made herself a piece of toast with some butter on and sat down at the wooden table.

She took her first bite, crunching being heard from her

teeth as Celestal munched away on the butter soaked toast. She ate the rest, while daydreaming out the window at the lush, chartreuse grass.

It was her first day of being an actual princess! Once she had finished eating her slice of toast, she grabbed her parents and rushed out the cottage door.

"*Where are we going*?" asked her parents. "*To the Cloud Castle, for my Coronation*," replied Celestal. Her parents realised all new princesses need to be crowned at a coronation event and it was their daughters special day today.

They all quickly galloped across the glades, making sure they were on time. Once they arrived, a guard appeared at the front gate of the castle.

"*Hello. You must be Princess Celestal, we are expecting you. I know it's your coronation day at which you are to be crowned princess of kindness. Come in*," the guard said. So the three clopped into the castle courtyard.

Celestal was led to the dressing room to get changed, whilst her parents made sure she was ok before leaving to journey back home to get ready. Once Celestal was seated, a royal hairdresser entered the room and began braiding her hair and hooficurering her hoofs.

Next, Celestal put on a huge, flowing, white dress that shimmered in the sunlight. One of the designer ponies, Sugar Sweet, thought it was beautiful!

Celestal said "*thank you for the compliment*". Celestal trotted to the door leading from the room where a castle pony was opening the door for her. "*Celestal, this is your big moment are you ready*?" the castle pony asked.

Celestal really was. It was scary, but she knew it would be fine. "*Yes, I can't wait*, " replied Celestal.

Queen Titana came over and led Celestal to a royal looking curtain. Queen Titana parted the curtain and swiftly popped outside onto the balcony that looked out over the crowds of ponies waiting to see the new princess. "*Attention everypony*!" the Queen announced in her royal Queen voice. Everypony fell silent.

"*We are about to start the coronation event that will crown the new royal: Princess Celestal*!" Every being cheered with a very large roar as the curtains opened and Celestal trotted out of the curtain archway and onto the balcony.

Queen Titana was with Celestal. And once they were at the front, the Queen stood behind the podium that held Celestal's crown.

"*I place this worthy crown on Celestal's head, and let it be known now that Celestal is now princess of kindness*!" exclaimed Queen Titana.

Her parents cried with happiness for their daughter. Everyone else cheered and clapped.

Celestal's crown was now on her head, and it had a pink star jewel on the top. It was a golden colour. She felt so special. Just being a princess made her feel deep down inside, joyful.

Celestal made her way to the gazebo, where everypony in her magic class at school was singing a choir song for her. Celestal waved to her friends. They waved back at her.

All of them wanted wings like her, or a stunning, golden horn. But she was special and talented deep inside. Everyone loved the song. Afterwards, they all had some lunch. Celestal was particularly hungry, since she had only had a small breakfast.

She wandered over and sat next to her two best friends on a quiet picnic table in the far corner of the royal gardens. Her friends were called Viola and Amelia. The two were interested in Celestal's wings.

"*How did you get them*?" asked Viola. "*Are they made of real gossamer*?" asked Ameila. "*Girls, slow down and focus on your food*," said Celestal to them both.

"*But yes Amelia, they are made of real gossamer*." "*So they are*!" replied Amelia. "*But how did you get them*?" asked Viola. "*It's a very long story*," said Celestal.

"*I braved the journey through Neverfree forest, outwit three Gargoyle Falcons and climbed to the top of Mount Red Vine to save this wonderous island of ours from war*!"

"*Wow! That is a lot*!" the two chimed. "*It is*," said Celestal. "*I feel I have been so lucky, like it was kind of heaven sent*." "*We do as well*," the two friends agreed.

A small dapple of sunlight reflected on Celestal's crown, the jewel splitting the spectrum of light into the seven colours of the rainbow: red, orange, yellow, green, blue, indigo and violet. It looked elegant.

"*So what will you do now that you have those wings and the power of kindness?*" they asked.

"*When Unicorn Island Needs me, I'll be there, to be kind and help others whenever they need it!*"

Look Out For The Next Book In The Series ...

Coming Soon!

Also By Mia Kenyon…

Meet the Friendship Club: Lotus, Oona, Ketzie, Sapphire and Lani! These special birds belong to the beautiful area known as Puffin Island, where adventure and hope never ends! Birds Rock is a rock on Puffin Island located on Spellbound Shore. It is located behind a pool of Quicksand. If a bird held the rock's carved neck, and said where they wanted to go, the pool of quicksand would take them. This charming new series by the author of Unicorn Magic will enhance young hearts and will be a favorite forever.

Printed in Great Britain
by Amazon

79268088R00037